for Alfie

Chistmas 2023

Jonnh

and "Tiger"
xx

Dedication

To the real Miss Sweeting, my first teacher.

Thank You to the original Tiger McDoo,
and to the original Triplets. You know who you are.
You inspired this story.

First published in Great Britain in 2023 by Blackhall Publishing

A catalogue record for this book is available from the British Library

ISBN 978-1-913369-13-2

Illustrated with watercolours and coloured pencils

Printed and bound in the UK on FSC certified paper by
Martins the Printers, Sea View Works, Spittal
Berwick-upon-Tweed TD15 1RS
martins-the-printers.co.uk

The Trouble with Oscar

by
Miss Tiger McDoo

as told to *Jonnie Wild*

with illustrations by *Brita Granström*

Chapter One
Is that it?

'Is that it, Miss? That thing?' I say, pointing towards the rocks beyond the harbour wall. 'It can't be. On the TV news it was massive.'

'I'm sure it was enormous once, Tiger,' says Miss Sweeting. 'But it's shrinking every day.'

'So why are we bothering? I mean, we've walked all the way from school just to see a lump of ice that's smaller than a house. You said it would be really interesting. But it's not like the whole frozen North Pole has arrived, with wild animals and igloos and everything. That would be exciting. This is b for boring.'

'That is extremely rude, Tiger McDoo. Of course it's interesting. This is the first time ever that an iceberg has drifted this far south. The North Pole isn't as frozen as it used to be, and it's cracking up. I worry for the future of our planet. And so should you.'

'Well, I'm not worried about it,' I say, with a

big fake Ya w n.

'Well, I'm worried about you, Tiger McDoo,' says Miss Sweeting. 'I don't know what's come over you this term.'

'Well, you don't have to live with **them**,' I say, kicking gravel towards my two brothers. 'You're not a triplet, are you? I bet you don't have to share a bedroom with two disgusting boys. You should try it, then you'd know.'

'I am not a You, I am a Miss,' says Miss Sweeting. 'And Patrick and Henry are very nice boys.'

'Nice? You call them nice?'

'Right! That's enough!' says Miss Sweeting, and she turns towards the rest of our class. 'Form up into your pairs, children! We're going to walk to the end of the harbour wall to do something extra-ordinary. We are actually going to touch a piece of the

Frozen Arctic.'

The icy words make my ears all shiver-rr-y. 'But Miss, what if I don't want to –'

'No more ifs and buts, Tiger McDoo. You pair up with me.' And she takes my hand, squeezes it, and gives me one of those delicious smiles that you just can't argue with. If smiles could smell, hers would smell of butterscotch sauce.

'Trust me, Tiger,' she says. 'It will be exciting. You are really going to enjoy this.'

And I suppose I do. Except I get some poo on my shoe. Not dog poo. This is far more disgusting. A very strange colour, and a very weird smell.

Chapter Two

Fish fingers.

After school, Mum drives us up the ramp into the car park on the supermarket roof.

'Can't we park in the Mother-and-Baby section by the lift?' says Patrick. 'We could pretend to be babies.'

'You three don't need to pretend,' says Mum, **yanking** the handbrake.

'Mum, I want that Swiss cheese again,' says Henry.

'Don't I deserve even just one little *please?*' Mum **slams** the car door.

Patrick and Henry ignore her and rush into the lift.

'It's my turn to press the button,' says Patrick, pushing Henry out of the way.

'For goodness sake,' says Mum. 'What's the fuss? Tiger, you press the button, please. You boys take the fruit-and-veg list. And behave. I don't want them calling the manager, like last week. That was a **ghastly** experience I do not wish to repeat.'

I've never really looked at the buttons before. There is a 0 to go down to the supermarket and a 1 to come back up again. There is a third button, but it's got tape over it and a sign in spidery writing that says:

Whoever wrote it can't spell. Miss Sweeting would not be impressed.

'Tiger!' Mum is waving her hand in front of my face. 'Stop daydreaming!' She reaches over and presses the 0. 'Honestly, I do not know which of you three is the worst. You are wearing me out.'

I am absolutely not going to be the worst triplet today. I am going to be the best. Like I always am.

Last on my list are the frozen fish fingers. The boys hate them. They race past me pushing their trolleys.

'Urrrh, you and your disgusting fish fingers,' says Henry. 'You smell of fish.'

'And she's got a face like a fish,' says Patrick. 'Tiger McFish.'

I say nothing, but I make an extremely rude face to their backs as they disappear. I hate being a triplet, I really do.

The only way to reach up to the back of the freezer cabinet to get a Giant Family Box is to climb into my trolley and stretch out my arm – like this …

Then, something cold…
         grabs my hand…
                  and gives it a **tug.**

10

Chapter Three

Battered by a cod.

I scream, pull my hand away, and fall backwards into my trolley, which takes off down the aisle and tips me out into the fruit juices.

People crowd round and lift me up.

What happened? Are you all right, dearie?

The poor girl looks pale. Perhaps she fainted.

Is she breathing? Someone ought to give her the Kiss of Life.

I am too embarrassed to admit that I have been attacked by a box of frozen fish fingers, so I just say, 'I'm fine, honestly. Just a little accident.'

Anyway, I have a damp patch on my bum that smells of blueberry yoghurt, which is even more embarrassing.

So, I grab the trolley and head for the checkout.

'Tiger McDoo, I cannot believe it.' Mum is looking at the half-empty, half-squashed pot of yoghurt. 'My daughter, who I have brought up to have good manners shames me in public by eating a yoghurt we haven't even paid for yet – and with her fingers, for goodness sake.' She unloads my trolley into hers. 'Honestly, shopping with you three is absolutely–.'

'Mum, that's not fair – I didn't – I mean–' Then suddenly I remember. '**Mum, the fish fingers!**' I grab the empty trolley and dash off to frozen food.

I climb into the trolley, reach up, open the cabinet… and then I stop. And think. Is this sensible? Whatever grabbed my hand is still in there.

All those bags and boxes: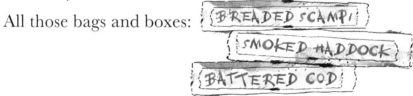

they all sound pretty fierce. I hope I'm not about to be battered by a cod.

So, I take a deep breath and reach into the back to snatch the Giant Family Box. But my fingers touch something – nothing breaded, smoked, or battered, but something soft and furry. And snoring!

I put my head into the cabinet, and there – fast asleep – is a small, white polar bear.

The polar bear opens one eye, yawns, and grunts:

'GRR-oOo-ONG?'

I can tell straight away what it is saying:

'WHATEVER TOOK YOU SO LONG?'

Chapter Four

Big ugly teeth.

'What's your name?' growls the Polar Bear when I get him safely back to my bedroom.

'Don't I deserve even one little Thank You for rescuing you from the supermarket and smuggling you home under my coat?'

'I said: What's–Your–Name?' growls the bear.

'Tiger McDoo. What's yours?'

'Tiger McDoo? What kind of name is that?'

'Tiger? Well, my real name is Florence, but I hate it. Everyone calls me Tiger. I've got ginger hair, haven't I? And I've got really big teeth. Look!'

'If tigers look like you, I'm glad we don't have them in the **Frozen Ar-rrr-ctic**.' He puts his nose up against mine and I can feel the icy words going up my nostrils making my teeth chatter.

'Now, pass me that box of frozen fish fingers.' grunts the bear. 'I want a snack.'

'Don't I get a *please?*'

'We don't do *pleases* in the Frozen Arctic. We know what we want. We say what we want. We get what we want.'

'You haven't told me your name yet. Mister Rude, is it?'

'Actually, it's Oscarrr.'

'Oscar who? What's your surname?'

'We don't do surnames in the Frozen Arctic. Don't need to. We don't go around in crowds. We live a solitary life. I'm the only Oscar-rrr between here and the North Pole.'

'But what about penguins? They go around in crowds. They must have surnames.'

'Penguins? They come from the Frozen South Pole, stupid! We wouldn't allow such pathetic creatures in the Frozen Arctic. I mean, penguins can't think for themselves. They waddle around in great big herds, wearing identical feathers, making the same daft clucking noises. No personality. No individuality. Boring. They wouldn't survive for ten minutes in the Frozen Arctic. Nor would you, even though you have big ugly teeth.'

'That was horrible. I don't know why I bothered to rescue you.'

'You didn't rescue me, stupid! I decided to come and live with you. All day I've been crouching in the freezer cabinet on the lookout for the perfect family to live with – you know: very rude, shocking manners and extremely grumpy, like all of us who live in the Frozen Arctic. This house is going to feel just like home. I chose you, Tiger McDoo. Now leave me alone. I want my nap.'

I can hear Patrick and Henry racing up the stairs to the attic bedroom we all share, so I throw my dressing gown over Oscar. I want to keep him a secret for now. He may be rude, but he chose *me*. He actually chose *me*.

Chapter Five

He bites!

'Hey, what's that lump on your bed?' says Henry, bouncing onto his bed.

'It's a lump-osserus!' says Patrick, somersaulting onto his bed. 'Or a lumpy-phant!'

'It's a lumpy-saurus rex! A dino-lump!' yells Henry jumping onto my bed and snatching my dressing gown. 'Hey! It's a lump of fur!'

'Actually,' I say, calmly. 'Actually, it's a polar bear. And you'd better stop prodding him, or he will bite you.'

'Oh yeah,' says Patrick, joining in the prodding. 'Your cutesy-wootsy toy bear is going to bite me? Well, I'm going to bite it first. On the nose. Oh yuck! It smells of fish.'

'Actually, he's been eating fish fingers. And he's not an It. He's a He, and He's called Oscar. Now leave us

17

alone. He's sleeping, and I'm thinking.'

'He's a roly-polar-lump!' says Patrick rolling Oscar off the bed and onto the floor. 'Hey, he's very heavy for a cuddly-wuddly toy.'

'I told you already; he's been eating. Buzz off! We want peace and quiet, like in the Frozen Arctic.'

'Wake up Oscar-lump!' says Henry, hitting Oscar with a slipper. 'Anyway, where did you get him from?'

'I didn't get him. He got me. Oscar found me. At the supermarket.'

'Oh deary-dear, Tiger' says Patrick, prodding Oscar again. 'Your fluffy-wuffy super-market cuddles is D-E-D – dead.'

'Yes,' says Henry, lifting Oscar's paw and letting it drop to the ground with a thump. 'I agree. His batteries are dead flat. Trust our girly-whirly Florence to bring home a smelly, dead toy.'

'I am N–O–T– not called Florence!' I yell, throwing slippers and books at them. 'Get – out – of – here – now!'

And all this time, Oscar has been motionless,

speechless, lifeless…

I lie down next to him and listen for his breathing, but he's breath-less, too.

Does that mean Oscar really is…

… dead?

I hear the boys laughing downstairs.

I curl up in a ball next to the dead bear and howl.

Even my tummy is crying.

Chapter Six

The kiss of life.

I can't get to sleep. Maybe the boys were right: the polar bear is just a toy. Maybe I was imagining … and then I remember …

The Kiss of Life!

That's what they do on TV, isn't it? I could try doing it to the bear.

So, I roll Oscar onto his back …

tilt his head back …

pinch his nose …

put my mouth over his …

and puff a kiss of life into him.

'Yucky-yuck-rrrrrr' roars the creature.

'What's that?' mumbles Patrick. Or Henry.

'It's just Oscar trumping,' I hiss. 'Go back to sleep!'

'You and your stupid lump of fluff. Go back to sleep

yourself!'

I take Oscar down to the bathroom for a wee, and to talk. He's never been in a bathroom before.

'You can either sit on the loo like me, Oscar, or stand up and do what Patrick and Henry do – but without the mess!'

But, what with him being a bit small, neither way seems to work, so I put him in the bath and he wees down the plughole.

'Ah, that's better,' he snorts.

'Now wash that yucky kiss out of my mouth.'

'Don't be so rude, Oscar. I've just brought you back to life. Don't I deserve just one little–'

'Brought me back to life?' grunts Oscar. 'I wasn't dead. I was just hibernating, stupid.'

'Hibernating? You mean – like – go to sleep for months at a time?'

'In the Frozen Arctic I'd dig a snow-hole and hibernate all winter if there was no food about.'

'So, when you look dead, you're not really dead?'

'Exactly. I slow down my breathing almost to nothing, so I don't burn any energy. The only way of telling whether I'm alive or dead is the Mirror Trick.'

'The Mirror Trick?'

'You hold a mirror in front of my nose. It will go foggy if there's even a tiny breath. But don't tell those revolting brothers of yours. Let them think I'm a cuddly toy.'

'So, you being alive is just our secret?'

'That's right. One rude, grumpy, bad-mannered McDoo is quite enough company.'

I'm about to say something rude back, but − you know − I'm glad that Oscar is actually alive again. 'Is there anything you want right now?'

'I want seal! Seal steak ... Seal sandwiches... Seal sausages... Anything,

as long as it's seal!'

Chapter Seven
In the fridge.

'No seal?' Oscar looks disappointed. 'Just put me in the fridge then. I want to cool down.'

I squeeze him in between the cheese and a chocolate cake.

'Oscar, listen!' I say, in my sternest Miss Sweeting voice. 'You are being really **ghastly**.'

'**Ghastly**?' says Oscar. 'What does that mean?'

'I'm not sure. Mum says it all the time. It's definitely something very bad. And that's what you are.'

'Huh, it's you who's ghastly. You and the rest of the McDoo family. **Ghastly**. I love that word!'

'No, we're not ghastly. And I'm definitely not.'

'Yum!' says Oscar, plunging a paw into a blueberry yoghurt. 'Nice yoghurt this; fancy the last one yourself?'

No sooner am I eating the yoghurt than Oscar points at me.

'Told you so: **ghastly** shocking manners. Look at you! Eating yoghurt with your fingers. And you should have offered the last one to me.'

'My manners are no worse than yours, and that was a stupid trick.'

'There you go: **ghastly** rude. I'm a guest in your house. You're supposed to be nice to me and get me everything I want. And I want more frozen fish fingers before I go back to bed.'

'You want this, you want that. What about me? What about what I want?'

'Hey-hey, **ghastly** grumpy girl! You'd fit in perfectly in the Frozen Arctic!'

'Why don't you just go back to the Frozen Arctic where you belong?' I snap, and I kick the fridge door shut.

'I can't,' says a very small voice. 'I can't.'

I open the door. There are tears in Oscar's eyes. I put my hand out and stroke him. 'You can't? But you're magic. You must be.'

Oscar lets out a tummy-wobbling laugh. I slam the fridge door again. The fridge w o b b l e s with laughter.

I open the door and there is something gooey running down Oscar's head.

'Nice eggs these,' says Oscar licking his lips. 'Not as nice as Glaucous gulls' eggs, but they'll do. Magic, did you say? I may have Special Instincts – like for smelling seals under the ice, but I'm no more magic than you are.'

'But … but how did you get here?' And then I remember. 'Of course! You were stuck on that iceberg that crashed into the harbour wall, weren't you?'

'And now I'm stuck here until there's a gale-force wind from the south to blow me back north. That doesn't happen very often. I might have to wait years and years in your bedroom.'

'But won't you grow to be huge and fierce?'

'Not if I don't have proper polar bear food.'

'Well, what's wrong with fish fingers and blueberry yoghurt? And we've got ice cream.'

'That's all very nice for a snack,' says Oscar, yawning, 'but it only keeps me going for an hour and then I have to hibernate.'

'Have you ever actually caught a seal, Oscar?' Oscar doesn't answer. He falls out of the fridge and into my arms, and I carry the snoring bear up to bed. He must be having a nice dream because he actually licks my cheek. The rude, grumpy bear…

actually… licks me!

Chapter Eight

Keeping a secret.

I come downstairs yawning.

Dad holds out a crushed chocolate cake covered in broken eggshells and blueberry yoghurt. 'Who raided the fridge last night? And left the freezer lid open? I know it was you, Tiger McDoo. Your bed is full of crumbs, and you stink like a fish. What do you think this is – a hotel? And if you don't hurry up, you'll be late for school. That goes for you boys as well. Stop hitting Patrick, Henry. Come on Team McDoo, come on.'

I put my hands over my ears. I hate it when Dad calls us triplets the Team. I am Tiger, not a team. Who would want to be in a team with Patrick and Henry? And it's all so unfair. The crumbs aren't mine. Oscar said not to worry, he would lick the duvet clean; but he's so messy. And the bum-print on the cake – well that was Oscar, too.

'Did you hear your father, Tiger?' Mum joins in now. 'Dad and I have jobs to go to. How do you think we keep you fed and clothed and in a house big enough for triplets. Tiger, are you listening?'

'You have precisely seven minutes, Team McDoo,' says Dad. 'And then we – and you – are leaving this house. Come on Team, I'm counting!'

Welcome to another **ghastly** day in the ghastly McDoo household.

Oscar is right; we are ghastly. Going to school is almost a relief. Except I am in the same class as my horrible brothers. There's no escaping them.

Walking to school I lag behind the boys, but the slower I walk the slower they walk. Then they turn and start walking backwards so they can see me.

'Good game this, Tiger,' says Patrick.

'It's not a game. I'm thinking,' I say. 'I need space.'

'What for?' says Henry

'You wouldn't understand; you two are just babies.'

'No, we're not,' says Patrick. 'We're as tall as you are.'

'No, you're not. Come and stand back-to-back with me.'

'She's right,' says Henry, measuring the two of us with his hand. 'She's sprouting.'

'Well she's still the baby,' says Patrick. 'I mean, she's the only one who's got a cuddly toy.'

'Oscar is not—' I am about to say that Oscar is not a toy, he's real. Instead I say calmly, 'Well at least my cuddly toy isn't rude and bad-mannered like you two are.' Of course, Oscar is, but I'm not going to tell that to the boys.

'It would be cool if your Oscar was actually a real polar bear,' says Henry.

'Well, he's not. And that's a silly idea.'

'We could train him to eat teachers, – and Mister Wilson next door,' says Patrick.

'You're not training my polar bear to do anything. It's not real, got it?'

'It's pretty realistic though – your toy,' says Patrick. 'Nice and heavy. Do they do dinosaurs like that?'

'Nope. The bear was the last one. Didn't you see the sign by the checkout? – *Discontinued line: Half Price.*

Anyway, the sign also said: *Some parts may come loose. Not suitable for small children.* That means you two.'

'Let's see which parts of you come loose,' says Henry, tugging my arm hard. Henry is always hurting me. Patrick just hurts me with horrible words.

'Wouldn't it be great if real animals came on that iceberg?' says Henry, letting go. 'We could go hunting.'

'Not with Tiger, though,' adds Patrick. 'We'd leave her at home with her cuddly toys. It would be too scary.'

'You're the ones who are scary,' I say. 'You frighten away all my friends. They only come for tea once and that's it. They say it's too noisy and rough with you two bouncing around.'

'Well, you bounce about, too,' says Henry.

'Not anymore,' says Patrick. 'She's changed.'

The boys are still walking backwards with small steps when we get to Shelley the Lollipop Lady at the school crossing. She looks at me and shakes her head as Patrick and Henry waddle backwards across the road.

'I know, Shelley,' I say with a shrug. 'They're like a pair of penguins.'

Chapter Nine

They shoot polar bears, don't they?

'I want to go and see the iceberg,' grunts Oscar. He is sitting by the open bedroom window sniffing the wind. 'No good,' he growls – very quietly, because the boys are asleep. 'Three days, and still a westerly. No good at all. I told you I could be here for years waiting for a gale-force southerly. I want to go and check up on the iceberg anyway. Put your dressing gown on and let's go.'

'What now – in the middle of the night?'

'Yes, I'll be safe in the dark. If I was spotted, that would be it. Humans shoot polar bears, don't they?'

'They wouldn't shoot you, Oscar.'

'Oh yes they would. My mother told me. We have to be very careful when we are raiding explorer's tents for food. They have guns. If they catch us, they shoot us.'

'Don't they just run away? They wouldn't want to be

your next meal.'

'Us eat humans? No way! Not enough fatty blubber. Give me a whale or a seal any day.'

'Anyway Oscar, if grown-ups spotted you, they'd put you in a zoo, not shoot you.'

'What's a zoo?'

'A zoo? Well, in a zoo they would put you behind bars, like in a big cage but with your own swimming pool. I expect they'd put you next to the penguins, so you'd have company.'

'Penguins? I'm not going next to penguins! It would be worse than sleeping next to your **ghastly** brothers. That's it! We're going down to the harbour now while it's dark.'

I feel safe walking down Harbour Street in the dark with Oscar by my side. After all, he is a polar bear, and for a small bear he has a very fierce roar. Anyway, there is no-one about.

In the moonlight, the iceberg glistens. It looks even smaller than it did last week. We sit on the harbour wall eating blueberry yogurts and stare at it.

34

'How did you manage to balance on top of that Oscar? It's so shiny.'

'It's upside down. It must have tipped right over when we crashed. The other side was covered in deep snow. I dug a snow hole for shelter. Good job that's all under the water now. There was a lot of mess – fish bones and things. Would have given the game away. Now no-one knows I'm here.'

'Except me,' I say, and put my arm round Oscar. 'Miss Sweeting says that by the end of term the iceberg will have melted to nothing.'

'That's what's happening in the Frozen Arctic,' grunts Oscar. 'It's getting too warm. The ice melts too much in summer and doesn't freeze enough again in winter. How can we hunt for seals when there's no ice to walk on? Polar bears are starving and it's not fair. What have we done to deserve it?'

'But you still want to go back, Oscar? You still want to look out for a wind from the south?'

'Of course I want to go back home, stupid. I don't want to be stuck behind bars in one of your zoos listening to penguins yak-yak-yakking all day.'

'You could stay with me.'

'Huh, and what would I do with all my polar bear's Special Instincts – you know, my incredible hearing instinct, my amazing smelling instinct for sensing a seal swimming deep under the ice?'

'You know, Oscar, there are seals living further out on the rocks over there. We could go seal hunting.'

But Oscar isn't listening. He's fallen asleep on my lap.

Poor Oscar. I don't think he's big enough to catch a seal. I'll just have to build up his strength with fish fingers. Or find some seal sausages.

Chapter Ten

That dangerous beast.

'Do we really have to go and see the iceberg tonight, Oscar?' We are sitting on top of our big stone gatepost eating blueberry yoghurts. I'm yawning already. Worn out.

'I need to go. I want to go. I will go,' grunts Oscar. 'And you've got to come with me.'

I think he's homesick. Every night we raid the fridge and the freezer before we set off down to the harbour. Oscar just likes to sit there and talk about the Frozen Arctic. It does sound really frightening. Oscar says everything in the Frozen Arctic is either an enemy, or food, or both. 'So don't blame me if I don't trust your brothers or your parents – or any **ghastly** human,' he says. 'Trust no-one. That's one of my Special Instincts.'

I daren't tell him that Miss Sweeting says that we

humans are responsible for the melting ice cap. All those lorries carrying plastic pots of blueberry yoghurt to the supermarket. And all those forests we keep chopping down. I do tell him that cows are responsible for a lot of global warming. 'They **trump** smelly methane gas like nobody's business,' I say.

Oscar grunts. 'You obviously haven't smelt a muskox trumping.'

'Well, I have to clear your smelly droppings out of the bath. Nothing could be worse than that.'

'Stop complaining. That's your job – to look after me.'

'At least you could say one little *thank you*. And I'm not your mother.'

'Mother? What do I need a mother for? If I hadn't got separated from my mother, I'd be leaving her soon anyway. We're not like you, living at home for years and years. We go off on our own before we're even two.'

'But you're too small to be on your own. You're still a baby!'

'I am not! I am–' Suddenly Oscar sniffs, stiffens, and puts a paw over my mouth. 'Someone's coming,' he whispers. 'Can't see them yet, but I can smell 'em.' He buries himself under my dressing gown. A torch shines in my face.

'What are you doing up there?' says a voice. 'Good job I'm a policeman and not that dangerous beast that's escaped off the iceberg. This your house?'

I hold Oscar very tight to me. I can't answer. I just look straight ahead. I am **terrified**. How did they find out about Oscar?

'Aren't you going to say anything? A minute ago you were chattering away to yourself.'

I don't answer.

'Come on, young lady, reach out and jump into my arms. I'll catch you,' says the policeman.

I don't move. I just keep on staring ahead, arms folded, hugging Oscar to my tummy under my dressing gown.

'You don't want to jump?' says the policeman. 'I'll have to come up there and get you then.'

I keep staring ahead. Out of the corner of my eye I can see the policeman climbing onto the wall by the gatepost and shuffling along until he is next to me. He grabs hold of me and lowers me to the ground, then jumps down himself.

'Take my hand, young lady, and let's go and ring the bell and see if this is your house,' he says.

I keep my arms folded.

'No need to be frightened,' he says. 'But you need to be inside, young lady, not out here with a **dangerous beast** running wild.'

I keep staring ahead and shuffle, a bit like a penguin,

towards the front door.

He rings the doorbell. Dad opens the door. I stare straight ahead and shuffle past him and up the stairs. It's not easy walking with your arms folded and a bear clinging to your tummy.

'My daughter must be sleepwalking,' I hear Dad say. 'We think she's been wandering about the house every night for weeks. She doesn't know what she's doing.'

'Thought so,' says the policeman. 'But she shouldn't be out on the street in the middle of the night.'

The voices disappear as I close the bedroom door. Patrick and Henry are asleep. I tuck Oscar up in my bed. They think he's a dangerous animal, do they? If only they could see him now. I slide under the bed and make myself as cosy as I can.

That was close! Oscar could at least have said *Thank you*.

Chapter Eleven

Have you heard the news?

'Have you all heard the news?' asks Miss Sweeting. 'I don't want to alarm you, but the police say there is an Arctic wolf roaming the streets. Mrs Tiffin says we are keeping all the playground gates shut. There is to be no playing in the field until the beast is caught.'

'Has anyone seen it?' asks Henry. 'I hope they are going to shoot it dead.'

'No-one has actually seen it, Henry,' said Miss Sweeting. 'They found some unusual animal droppings down by the harbour, close to the iceberg. The laboratory at the zoo identified them as Arctic wolf. That's how we know. And let's hope they don't shoot the poor creature.'

Everyone starts talking at once. I'm not listening. The zoo must have got it wrong. Oscar must have done a poo by the harbour wall. And now the police are hunting for a wild creature. With guns.

'Quiet please, children! Now while we are on the subject of Arctic animals, what other creatures live in the Arctic?'

'Miss, Miss!' says Martha Mizen. 'Penguins of course!' Martha is one of my friends who won't come round anymore because of Patrick and Henry. I'm not her friend anymore.

'Nonsense, Miss!' I say grumpily. 'Penguins live at the other end of the planet. In the Antarctic.'

'You're quite right, Tiger,' says Miss Sweeting. 'Penguins do live in the Antarctic.'

'And anyway, penguins are stupid, Miss. They're all the same. Go around in teams. No individuality. Boring.'

'That's a little unfair, Tiger. Now, does anyone know any other animals that live in the Arctic?'

'Miss, Miss, polar bears do. Especially cuddly-wuddly ones,' shouts Patrick, looking straight at me and laughing.

I stand up and stick my tongue out at Patrick.

'So do muskoxen, Miss,' I say, yawning. 'And reindeer and arctic foxes. Oh, and glaucous gulls. Their eggs are very tasty.'

'You seem to know a lot about the Arctic, Tiger, though I was not asking you,' says Miss Sweeting.

'So why are we going on and on when what I absolutely need to know is where to find seal sausages to go with the eggs, for goodness sake?'

Everyone laughs. Patrick shouts something about dead

bears. Miss Sweeting walks slowly towards me. She's left her butterscotch smile behind.

'Florence McDoo! That is extremely rude! Your bad manners and silliness are affecting the whole class. Go and stand outside Mrs Tiffin's office! I don't know what it is that's got into you, but you need help getting it out.'

Oh no! Miss Sweeting has gone **ghastly**, too.

Mrs Tiffin is the headteacher. At break, Miss Sweeting comes, and we go into the office together.

'Now, Florence,' says Mrs Tiffin. 'Miss Sweeting says you've become very rude and silly this term, and it's affecting the other children.'

I yawn. I put my hand over my mouth, but I do yawn. Mrs Tiffin gives me an icy stare.

'And the last week or so she's been yawning all the time,' adds Miss Sweeting. 'She can't stop. It's as if she never goes to bed.'

'Something really has got into you, young lady,' says Mrs Tiffin. 'Has something happened at home? Is that what's troubling you?'

'Yes – I mean no.' I start to cry. 'It's global warming, Mrs Tiffin. That's what it is. It's melting the icecap, and all the Arctic creatures are suffering and it's our fault and it's not fair.'

'You really mean that, don't you Tiger?' says Miss Sweeting handing me a tissue.

'I do. It's not fair. And then there's other things – things at home.'

'And you're worrying so much you can't sleep properly?' asks Mrs Tiffin. 'I think we should talk to your parents.'

'No don't do that,' I say firmly. 'I'll sort it myself. Whatever's got into me. I'll get it out. Just give me a bit of time.'

Chapter Twelve
I need help.

'Oscar, wake up! I need your help.'

'Well you can't have it. I'm sleeping.'

'I'm in trouble at school.'

'Good.'

'And I'm frightened.'

'Good.'

'I think I've caught an **infection**.'

'Serves you right. You eat with your fingers and never wash your hands first.'

'Miss Sweeting says now I'm **infecting** the whole class.'

'Good. Now leave me alone.'

'But Oscar, it's not my fault. I know I'm all the ghastly things you call me, but that's not really me. Something has got into me: an infection. I think it's either Mum or Dad that's in some kind of trouble and they've got infected first and brought it home. Both of them are really, really ghastly – and they never used to be. You could help me find out how the infection got into our house. You and me, we could be detectives - a team.'

'A team? Me and you?' Oscar puts his paws over his ears. 'You're kidding? I know your ghastly father calls you triplets The Team, but that doesn't mean I'm going to join in. I mean you three are just like penguins. You share the same bedroom, you talk the same, you dress alike and if it wasn't for your hair, you'd look alike. Yes, The Penguins. I'm going to call you that from now on.'

'I am not a penguin! I want to be me, just like you are you. I hate, hate, hate being The Team!'

'Well, what I want is to go down to the iceberg again,' grunts Oscar. 'Tonight!'

'Well, you can't, because what I want is that we do the detective work on the infection.'

'**Won't!**' growls Oscar.

'**Will!**' I growl back. I sound more like him every day.

'Tiger! What are you doing up there?' It's Mum,

shouting again. 'I've been calling for ten minutes. Don't I deserve even just one little answer? Your tea is stone cold.'

'See what I mean, Oscar?' I whisper. 'It's Mum who's infected.'

'Coming, Mum,' I shout, and I head downstairs chanting

'I am not a boring penguin …

        I am a detective…

            I am not a boring penguin…'

'Tiger McDoo, look at you,' yells Mum. 'You haven't brushed your hair again! You expect me to untangle it when it gets knotted, do you?'

'And where do you think your mother gets the time from to do that?' adds Dad, plonking down a plate of shrivelled sausages in front of me. 'You can't buy time in the supermarket.'

I pick up my knife and fork and push the sausages around the plate, looking downwards to hide my tears – and hide my secrets. I can't tell anyone about Oscar. And now I can't take him out at night because the police think he's a dangerous Arctic wolf. And I've got to keep that secret from Oscar because the poor thing will be terrified if I tell him that they are after him with guns. And all this time his iceberg is melting fast. And I can't tell Miss Sweeting and Mrs Tiffin why I am yawning. And Mum and Dad think I am sleepwalking. And they are making everything worse because they are **infected** with something. And that's where I've got to start my Detective work, on my own, in secret.

'I'm sticking this up on the fridge,' says Dad. 'Just so you don't forget.'

It's a flyer that was shoved through the letterbox. From the police.

WHAT TO DO IF YOU SEE THE ARCTIC WOLF.

I stab a sausage. I don't know whether to laugh or cry.

Chapter Thirteen
Behind bars!

'Pssst! Tiger!' comes a whisper from under my bed.

'Shut up, Oscar! I'm trying to sleep!' For the first time in days, I'm sleeping in my bed. Oscar's actually volunteered to sleep on the floor.

'Come down here! I've decided I want to be a detective, too.'

'You said I was a boring penguin, not a detective. You said…'

'Yes, but this is exciting! If I lie with one ear to the floor, I can hear your parents down below in their bedroom talking about something very suspicious.'

'Oscar, we shouldn't be listening when they're having a private conversation.'

'Do you want my help or don't you? There's no such thing as a private conversation in the Frozen Arctic.'

I'm not sure whether Frozen Arctic Rules apply in my bedroom. But it's cold under my bed, so it's sort of Arctic conditions. I put my ear to the floor. 'I can't hear anything.'

'Well, no wonder,' whispers Oscar. 'You don't have Special Hearing Instincts, like me.'

'I know, I'll do what detectives and special agents do. I'll put a glass on the floor and my ear on the glass.' I grab the water glass from my bedside table. 'Hey, Oscar, it works! I can hear them now.' But somehow it doesn't seem right for me to be listening, so I just leave it to Oscar. 'What are they saying, Oscar? Tell me!'

'Shhhhh! I've gone and missed that bit. And now your Mum has started crying, so I can only catch a few of his words. Yes, I can hear…

… Caught by police … Blood on hands … Big trouble … Locked up …

… Never ever again."

Now he's gone downstairs to make a cup of tea. But he's definitely in **big trouble**. No wonder he's so grumpy.'

'Dad? In **big trouble?**' I shout, but I'm shaking so much that all that comes out of my mouth are a few wobbly hisses. Oscar understands.

'Sounds like it.' he says, casually, popping a fish finger into his mouth. ' **Ghastly**, isn't he?'

'Did … did … did he say that the Police found him with blood on his hands and he'll be locked up behind bars and never ever let out?'

'That's what he said. There was another bit about blueberry yogurt. I'm pretty sure that was your father

54

asking the policeman if he would be allowed blueberry yogurt in prison, and the policeman said: what was your Dad expecting, *Waiter Service?*'

'But what's Dad done?'

'He didn't say. He was rather casual about it all, so I expect he's done it lots of times before. **Ghastly** people are always going round doing **ghastly** Crimes.'

'No, Oscar, Dad was a lovely Dad until recently. This must have been his very first crime. I'm sure he didn't really mean to do it.'

'Doesn't matter whether he meant it or not. Sounds like he expects to be locked up anyway. And good riddance! One less **ghastly** McDoo means more food for me.'

'Oscar, don't say that!' I hiss.

I crawl back into bed, but I don't sleep much. My jumbled feelings are tumbling around inside me, and they've got sharp corners, so I can't get comfortable.

What are we going to do without Dad?

My Dad...

...in **big trouble**.

Chapter Fourteen

Big trouble.

Mum is cooking bollynaise. Chopping onions is making her cry. I start crying, too.

'Mum, what are we going to do when Dad goes to prison?'

'What are you talking about, Tiger?'

'He's in **big trouble**, isn't he? The Police have caught him with blood on his hands.'

Mum slams down her mug of tea. 'You think your father is in trouble with the Police? What on earth put that **ghastly** idea into your head, Tiger?'

'Mum, you can tell me the truth. I know he didn't mean to do it, but now he's going to be locked up behind bars.'

'For goodness sake Tiger, what's got into you? You

haven't been telling your brothers all this nonsense
have you?'

'Mum, what are we going to do? The Police are never
ever going to let him out again.'

'Tiger, what is happening to you? Your Dad is a
tired Dad, an exhausted Dad, a Dad at his wits' end,
but not a wanted-by-the police Dad. Trust me, I should
know: he's my husband. And you are my out-of-control
daughter!'

Either Mum is telling **the truth**, or she is a **very
good actor**.

And then I start howling, which is not acting
because I am out-of-control like Mum says. Even
when she takes me in her arms and whispers, 'Oh Tiger,
my Tiger, I'm sorry. You need help, and I'm no help at
all.'

Even wrapped inside Mum's hug, even with her being
kind and warm, and my face buried in her long hair
smelling of spaghetti bollynaise, and her tears tickling
my ear, even knowing that Dad is not in **big trouble**
with the Police, everything still feels icy cold inside me.

Mum was right; Miss Sweeting was right. I need help. And the bear in my bed is all the help I've got.

If it wasn't Dad, it must be Mum who's in **big trouble**. There's something that's got into her, and I know it's not her fault. I mean, she was the best Mum before. Now she can't help it: it's the infection. And I'm going to save her.

And I'll give that polar bear **one more chance** to show me that he really does have Special Instincts. If he gets it wrong again, I'll … I'll do something …

really…

    really…

ghastly!

Chapter Fifteen

Strictly private and confidential.

Oscar and I do a lot of detective spying on Mum, looking for clues.

Oscar is very helpful for a change. He has amazing Special Instincts! He teaches me how to crawl very quietly and curl up behind furniture just listening and smelling for clues. He also shows me how a polar bear makes himself completely invisible in the Frozen Arctic by covering his black nose with a white paw.

'See!' he says, proudly. 'Now I'm white from head to toe. If I stand next to a white wall you'd trip over me before you saw me.'

I'm getting rather tired of crawling round listening and smelling. Oscar is fed up and says he'd rather Mum stayed **ghastly** anyway. He creeps back to my bedroom to hibernate. I think Mum is beginning to suspect that we are using special instincts on her.

'Tiger, is that you hiding behind the sofa? Why are you following me around? Go out and play football with the boys. But don't leave the back yard; the police haven't found that wild beast yet.'

I don't answer. I put my hand over my nose, just like Oscar. I am invisible. I am in a snow-hole, like in the Frozen Arctic. No-one will find me. The Police will never find Oscar, either.

Then, I have a stroke of luck.

I am curled up in a ball behind the coats by the front door when I hear footsteps.

The postman! It starts raining letters, and I catch a whiff of something like disinfectant. Maybe someone has used disinfectant to wipe their fingerprints off an envelope.

Someone who wants to keep vital evidence from me. Very clever, but not clever enough to fool Detective McDoo. The disinfected envelope is big and white and addressed to Mum.

I've actually smelled a clue! Oscar will be proud of me. I take the envelope and rush up to our bedroom to show him.

'Oscar wake up, for goodness sake! I need your Special Instincts right now. Look at this! It's a letter from the Hospital. It has to be a …

very important clue!'

Chapter Sixteen

The envelope.

'Hmm,' grunts Oscar. 'We don't have many envelopes in the Frozen Arctic. We don't have many postmen either. They're probably frightened of being bitten by a polar bear. Yuck, this smells! And you've actually stolen it? How **ghastly**!' Oscar sounds very pleased.

'No, I'm just borrowing it. And I'm doing it for Mum's Own Good. I need to get into this envelope and read the letter without Mum knowing I have.'

'It looks like a very ordinary envelope to me,' says Oscar.

'Am I the only proper detective round here, Oscar? Look what it says:

"STRICLY PRIVATE AND CONFIDENTIAL.
To be Opened by Addressee Only."

You see, Oscar, it must be **very important**, because it's not just "Private", it's "Private AND Confidential". And it's "STRICTLY" as well.'

'So, what's an "Addressee Only"?' says Oscar.

'I'm not sure, Oscar, but that sounds **very important** too.'

'And how do you know it's from the Hospital?'

'Look, here on the back; it says:

> *"If Undelivered, Return to Professor Pamela Catchpole, The General Hospital."*

It's not just a letter from a Doctor, it's a Professor. Like a letter from a Head Teacher. **Very important**, Oscar. No doubt about it. Now show me how to open it without Mum knowing!'

'We don't need to open it at all,' grunts Detective Oscar. 'With my Special Instinct for seeing seals hiding under ice, I can read the writing through the envelope.'

'Oscar, are you sure you can read?'

'At least as well as you,' says Oscar. 'It's just my

spelling that's a bit wobbly. We don't have much use for spelling in the Frozen Arctic. Sometimes even my breath freezes, so my growls and grunts come out all spiky and covered in ice, and clatter to the ground in broken pieces with all the letters jumbled up. Impossible to spell that mess. But this is easy.'

'Well, if you're sure, Oscar.'

'The first bit says: *"The symp-toms"*… something I can't read, then… *"a ser-ious-condition."* Then it says: something… *"com-plicati-ons"*; then the last bit is very clear. It says, *"Bring your husb-and as well as Tiger."* That's it. I can't see any more than that.'

'Oh, Oscar! Mum has ssss-symptoms!' I gasp for breath, but it feels like a snake has got in and is wedged in my throat.

'Sssss-she's got,' my snake-in-the-throat hisses, 'a sss-serious condition.'

I grab Oscar's paw and press it hard into my tummy. The words, the tears, the breath, and the snake come *tumbling out of my mu…*

'Oh, Os-ssss-car! Mum – her infection, it's a serious condition! And the Professor wants me and Dad to be there to comfort her when he tells her that she's getting complications! My Mum! Oscar, are you sure?'

'Of course I'm sure. My Special Instincts are never wrong. Now stop crying and go and get me some ice cream. I want it now!'

But I'm crying so much I can't move. Not for Oscar. Not for anybody.

Chapter Seventeen

I need to know the truth.

'Dad, I need to know the truth.' I say to Dad when I catch him on his own. 'When is Mum going into hospital?'

'What a funny question, Tiger. Mum is very healthy.'

'But Dad, that's not true! She's got an infection with symptoms and a serious condition!'

'Tiger, this is nonsense. You haven't been upsetting The Team with this, have you?'

'But Dad, it is true! And now she's getting complications! She's not going to die, is she?'

'But Tiger, what if—'

'Dad there's no time for ifs and buts! What about the Kiss of Life? That works, I absolutely know. Dad, please, can we try that?'

'Tiger, calm down and listen.'

'Listen? There's no time to listen. The Professor at the Hospital. Her letter, she's going to tell her – tell us. She's nearly–'

'Stop it Tiger! That's enough! Look at me! It's true, Mum is worried. It's true, Mum is worn out. It's true, she has not been herself lately. It's true, none of us have been ourselves lately. But Mum does not have Symptoms, or a Serious Condition, or Complications. Mum does not have an infection of any kind; Mum is just worn out!'

'But the appointment at the Hospital. Is that to get medicine for being Worn Out?'

'Tiger, the only appointment at the Hospital is nothing to do with Mum. It's to do with … well, Mum and I are going to talk to you about it tomorrow. Trust me Tiger, Mum is not poorly. You've just got confused about something, what with you being so tired and … well, just come here and let me give you a big hug. You poor thing, Tiger. Come on, let me wipe your eyes.'

But I can't stop crying. And thinking: that stupid, know-all polar bear who thinks his Special Instincts are always right! Fancy telling me Mum was infected when she wasn't. And that Dad is in **big trouble**, when he isn't.

Revenge. A really Ghastly revenge. I don't know what it is yet, but whatever it is, that Ghastly polar bear deserves it.

Chapter Eighteen
The ghastly revenge.

Oscar's hiding under my duvet. He knows he's done wrong.

He'll have to come out eventually. He'll want fish fingers. He'll want ice cream. He'll want, want, want.

I lie on the floor waiting for him. If a gale blowing from the south never happens, he could still be living in my bed when I'm grown up. If he's going to stay, I need to teach him a lesson he'll never forget. Trouble is, I'm not very good at revenge. Maybe he will apologise, then I won't have to do it.

'Patrick? Henry?' I whisper. I'm going to tell them everything. I can't keep the truth about Oscar a secret for a moment longer. But Patrick and Henry are asleep.

I feel Oscar's hot breath in my ear.

'What do you want now, Oscar?'

'I want a wee. Oh, and after that I want–'

'Shut up Oscar! And you can start by apologising.'

'Yes, I want a whole tub of ice cream, and blueberry yoghurt of course.'

I prod him with Henry's cricket bat. 'Oscar, I've got a gun!'

'So, you're going to shoot me, are you? Well, that's typical of you **ghastly** McDoos. You invite a guest into your house, and then you shoot him.'

'I didn't invite you,' I hiss. 'You invited yourself.'

'As far as I'm concerned, I am a guest and I want–'

'Shut up Oscar! I bet you brought that infection all the way from the Frozen Arctic. Everything was alright until you turned up.'

'No it wasn't. You were already rude and grumpy. And miserable.'

'Well, I'm miserable now.' I say, and suddenly I realise what it must be like to be Mum. Oscar has worn me out. 'Very, very miserable. I can't live with you anymore, Oscar.'

'You mean you're leaving home, Tiger?'

'No, you are leaving, Oscar. I can't cope with keeping you secret, and then all the time you are so mean.'

'You're the one who is mean. I pity your poor brothers.'

'For goodness sake shut up Oscar! Now listen, I've decided to tell Mum and Dad about you. It's not safe here. The Police are looking for you. You'll be safer in a zoo. That southerly gale is never going to start blowing.'

'You never know, Tiger. Open the window and let me smell the breeze.'

Oscar climbs onto the windowsill and starts sniffing.

'You know Tiger, I think this is going to be my lucky night.'

I am getting crosser and crosser.

'The wind is not going to change, Oscar. Like you are never going to change. I mean it, it's the end of our secret.'

'Tiger, the wind; I'm serious. Smell it!'

'And I'm serious too, Oscar! I really am going to tell Mum and Dad. You need to be in a zoo – for your **own good**. Safely behind bars.'

'Well, I'm leaving then,' snorts Oscar. 'The sooner the better. In fact, if you want me to leave, I'll go right now.'

'You go then, Oscar, and good riddance!' I snort back. I'm crying; this is not how I wanted revenge to be.

And that's when it happens. Oscar leaps off the windowsill with the kind of leap that only a polar bear with a Special Instinct for chasing seals across broken ice could do.

And he lands in the old monkey puzzle tree which reaches right up to our attic bedroom window.

'Oscar! I didn't mean it!' I yell as he tumbles down through the spiky branches. He comes to a stop on a branch overhanging the road. It starts to bend.

'Oscar, come back! Please, come back!' There's a loud crack and the branch breaks. Oscar falls with a thump into the road and lies there motionless.

'I'm coming Oscar! I didn't mean it!' I scream.

I run downstairs to the front door. The key isn't in the lock, but I know where they hide it. In the vase. Except it isn't there. Why do they keep moving it? Ah, there it is,

on top of the mirror.

'Oscar, I'm coming!'

Oscar is still lying in the middle of the road. I run towards him.

'Back, Tiger-rrrr, back!' Oscar lifts his head.

'The carrrrrr!'

I remember bright headlights. I remember the squeal of brakes. I remember the squeal of Oscar as the car hits him. And did I squeal, too?

And then I am lying in Dad's arms, feeling I am starting to hibernate.

'Oh, Tiger, Tiger, Tiger,' he is saying. 'Oh, Tiger.'

Chapter Nineteen
The pink professor.

I know Miss Sweeting is crying because I can feel her tears running down my neck as she hugs me.

'And that's the end,' I tell her. 'The trouble with Oscar is ... he's dead. It's not Mum who was going to die. It's Oscar. And it's not Dad who should be locked up behind bars. It's me. **Ghastly**, **ghastly** me!'

She takes me to the cloakroom. Mum and Dad are coming to collect me early. She has to help me on with my coat because my left arm is in plaster. Did I tell you that the car hit me?

This time we are not going to the hospital to see about my broken arm. We are going to see Professor Catchpole about my **ghastlyness**.

'You won't need your gloves on, Tiger. That wind from the south is still blowing a gale, but it's a warm wind. It's

melted that iceberg almost to nothing.'

'That doesn't matter anymore,' I mumble. 'And Miss, please don't tell Mum and Dad about Oscar. I don't want them to know that I kept a secret from them. They'll think I didn't trust them. Best if everyone thinks he was a fluffy toy.'

'You can trust me, Tiger,' says Miss Sweeting, wiping her eyes with her hanky. Then she wipes my wet cheeks, and I can smell the sweet butterscotch tears that go with her butterscotch smile. 'Your lovely, grumpy Oscar was a fluffy toy.'

Except Oscar isn't fluffy any more. When they came to visit me in hospital, Henry told me he had found Oscar at the roadside. 'Your bear thing was a complete mess,' he said.

'I told him to put it in the dustbin,' said Patrick.

'I haven't,' said Henry. 'I was going to put it in the washing machine for you, but I've left it on the boiler to dry out instead.'

I've hardly stopped crying since. I didn't know I could have so many tears inside me.

I try not to cry when we go in to meet the Professor. Mum and Dad are upset enough already without me dripping tears.

'Do you know why you are here, Tiger?' asks the Professor. I like her pink dress.

'Because I have the **ghastly** infection.'

'Really? And what kind of symptoms do you have?'

I don't answer. I'm thinking about my revenge that went wrong, and how Oscar was trying to tell me that the wind was changing, and how he could be back in the Frozen Arctic by now. Except his dead body, all battered and filthy, is shut in the boiler cupboard. I can't bear to go and look at him. Dead. And it's my fault.

'Tiger?' The Pink Professor is stroking my arm. 'You've gone very quiet. I asked you about your symptoms.'

'Oh? Yes, well, **ghastly** rudeness, **ghastly** bad manners and **ghastly** grumpiness.'

'Dear oh dear, Tiger, that sounds like a serious condition,' says the Pink Professor. 'But that's not why you are here today. It's more complicated than that.

You see, every night for the last few weeks you have been wandering round the house fast asleep. Your Mum and Dad keep finding you in all sorts of strange places. They've been getting up every night for weeks on end, and they are suffering from Exhaustion, and don't know what to do, which is why they have asked me to help.'

Then Dad starts at me: 'Tiger, don't you realise what you get up to every night?

Emptying the freezer…
leaving the fridge door open…
weeing in the bath…
wandering in the garden… '

I put my hands over my ears. I don't want to hear all this, but there's no stopping Dad.

'The other night a policeman saw you balancing on the gatepost. He rushed over and managed to help you down. When he rang the doorbell, he was very angry, even when I told him you were sleepwalking. He said you were bleeding, and held up his blood-stained hands, but it was only blueberry yoghurt. Yoghurt or no yoghurt, he said; if we allowed our children to do this sort of thing in the middle of the night, he was going to report us to Social Services. Said we should control you properly, like proper parents, or we'd be in big trouble. I said what are we supposed to do, lock you up and put bars on the windows and keep you imprisoned and never, ever let you out again?'

Mum looks at me with worn-out tears in her eyes. 'I know you were asleep Tiger, but you must remember something, don't you?'

I don't know whether to say yes or no. I don't know what's the right thing to do. Keeping so many secrets has got me in a muddle.

'Poor Oscar,' I say. 'He's dead and it's my fault. I'll never see him again. My best friend ever, ever.'

'Oscar?' says Dad.

'Who's Oscar?' asks Mum.

The Pink Professor takes my hand. 'I would like to have a heart-to-heart with Tiger. On my own. Why don't you two wait in the canteen – get yourselves a cup of tea?'

Chapter Twenty

The trouble with Oscar

'Now Tiger, I would like to hear all about your friend Oscar.'

'I don't want to talk about Oscar.'

'Your parents don't seem to know about this friend of yours. Was he such a special friend that you had to keep him a secret?'

'Yes, that's it, the trouble with Oscar…' And before I realise what I am doing, I'm telling her all about him and his grumpiness, and the iceberg and the southerly wind, and why I had to keep him a secret in case he was sent to the zoo. 'And the police said he was a dangerous Arctic wolf,' I say laughing. 'But you should have seen him all curled up in my bed, stuffing himself with frozen fish fingers!'

The Pink Professor laughs, too.

'So why do you think this lovely, well-mannered Miss Tiger McDoo has not been herself lately? Was it all grumpy Oscar's fault?'

'It's all my fault. Oscar always said I was the ghastliest. I didn't realise that he was right, until … he died. He was running away from me and my stupid revenge.'

'Tiger, this feeling **ghastly** – Miss Sweeting is sure that you haven't been bullied,' says the Pink Professor. 'And your Mum and Dad say that there's been nothing upsetting at home. Mum, Dad, your brothers you're all together, one family…'

'But that's it!' I croak, tears pouring down my cheeks. 'One family, one team, but **not** one **me!** When I want to be just me, Mum and Dad just get cross with me. I'm not a penguin like Oscar said, and it's not fair because I am sensible, and I am different, and I'm not babyish like Patrick and Henry, and I want my own bedroom. And, I've got big teeth. And Florence is a horrible name. And then Osca–'

'Ah, Oscar, your friend Oscar,' says the Pink Professor, leaning closer.

'It was all right for him. In the Frozen Arctic everyone can just get on with being themselves. There aren't any Team McDoos in the Arctic. He's lucky. He *was* lucky.'

'And you're lucky, too, Tiger, aren't you? I think the shock of your accident has made all the family – even Patrick and Henry – realise how very special you are, and that you are growing up very fast into a wonderfully loveable Miss Tiger McDoo, the-one-and-only you.' She passes me another tissue. 'You know, it's all very well for Oscar living a solitary life in the Frozen Arctic, but you and I are not like that, Tiger. We need to be part of a team as well as being our one-and-only selves. Can you see that?'

'I suppose so,' I say, but I'm not sure.

'And it wasn't your fault he ran away and got run over. You weren't being cruel. It wasn't revenge. You were telling the truth. You couldn't cope any more with keeping him secret. You needed to make sure he was safe, because you loved him. And he loved you, too. From what you've told me, Oscar saved your life, didn't he?

He died trying to save you from being run over. Oscar is a Hero. I hope you gave him a Hero's Funeral.'

A Funeral? That's it! A proper Hero's Funeral. With flowers and speeches. Why hadn't I thought of that before?

The trouble with poor dead Oscar is … he needs a Funeral.

And I'm going to
give
him
the
biggest
and
best
funeral
– ever!

Chapter Twenty-one

The biggest and best funeral - ever.

Oscar's never had a bath before.

'If I ever want a bath – which I won't,' he growled when I suggested he get in the bath with me. 'I will immerse myself in icy water, the colder the better.'

Well, he can't argue any more. It's hot water, shampoo and conditioner for Oscar. You can't turn up filthy at your own funeral.

When he's all scrubbed up and clean, I leave him on the basin to dry off while I write a list for the Hero's Funeral.

1. Cardboard box for coffin.

2. Wreath of flowers from garden.

3. Fish fingers and blueberry yoghurt to put in coffin for journey to heaven.

4. Dig grave.

5. Bake buns (24) with sprinkles, for after.

6. Write invitations. Don't forget nice Pink Professor. And Miss Sweeting (who I have been awful to).

7. Ask P and H to make Hero's Medals and Badges of Courage.

8. Write Funeral Speech. Mum says it's called a Yolergee. It has to be very long and only say nice things about Oscar. That may be difficult.

9. Tissues for weeping mourners.

10. Black T-shirt and jeans. And my Halloween witch's hat.

11. Borrow big sunglasses from Mum to hide my tears.

12. Confetti? Or is that just for Weddings? Oscar would have liked confetti, so we'll have some.

When I get back up to the bathroom, Oscar is dry and fluffy.

But there is something rather odd.

Just above Oscar, the mirror behind the basin is

steamed up.

Very odd.

And then I remember something Oscar once said. 'The Mirror Trick'! Put a mirror in front of the nose and see if it steams up.

Oscar's not dead! Stuck in that hot boiler cupboard with no food for days, he's had to use his Special Instincts and hibernate!

OSCAR IS ALIVE!

I rush downstairs and put him in the freezer to cool down to Frozen Arctic temperature.

In the middle of the night, I wake up… and remember… and remember… Oscar!

He should have come out of hibernation by now.

I creep downstairs, open the freezer lid and peer inside.

Oscar is lying there floppy and still.

I was wrong. He really was dead. The Hero's Funeral will go ahead tomorrow as planned. Silly me to think he could still be alive. Still, I can't help crying.

I am just about to put down the lid, when the dead Polar Bear opens one eye, yawns and grunts:

'GRR-OOO-ONG?'
'WHATEVER TOOK YOU SO LONG?'

Chapter Twenty-two

Seal of quality

'Oh, my darling Oscar, my Hero Oscar!' I say, as I rock him in my arms.

'Yuck! What's all this luvvy-duvvy stuff?' grunts Oscar. 'Can't you just be **ghastly**?'

'Oh, Oscarrrrr,' I weep.

'Stop purring like a pussycat. What I want is a picnic! No, a feast! And I want it now!'

How can I possibly refuse my hero anything? So, I spread yesterday's newspaper out on the kitchen table and pile the entire contents of the freezer in the middle.

Of course, Oscar doesn't offer to help even though I've got one arm in plaster.

'Hey, Tiger, what have you done to your arm?'

'I was hit by that car. You saved my life, remember?'

'Doesn't sound like me at all. Polar bears' Special

Instincts don't include saving lives. We just look out for ourselves. I must be going soft.'

'Well you did, Oscar. Don't you remember anything?'

'I remember sitting on the windowsill and my nose twitching. Yes, that was it. I sensed the wind was changing. And then… I think we were both very angry… I was bouncing through a spiky tree and my Special Instincts were telling me that this is not a good thing for a polar bear to do and I'd better go into hibernation. So I did.'

'Oscar,' I say, nervously. 'The wind did change. We've had a gale-force southerly.'

'What?' groans Oscar. 'I've missed a southerly. What will the others say?'

'What others?'

'Never you mind,' growls Oscar. 'I'll just have to hope they didn't launch The Iceberg without me.'

'But the iceberg you came on has melted.'

'So what?' growls Oscar, dipping a fish finger into the blueberry yoghurt.

'Oscar, you know what? Mum and Dad have agreed to

divide our big attic bedroom into two bedrooms, one just for me – and you now, of course. Isn't that brilliant?'

'**Ghastly**' grunts Oscar.

'And soon I'm going to get a brace with pink sparkly bits so my teeth don't stick out so much. And what about my new hairstyle? Don't you think it's cool now it's all untangled and short?'

'**Ghastly**,' grunts Oscar. 'It's all right for you. You haven't missed a gale-force southerly. You don't need seal meat to make you grow up big and … and …'

Oscar is staring at the newspaper spread out in front of him.

'Well I never!' He brushes away fish finger crumbs. 'Look, an advert for the supermarket: *New Improved Premium Sausages.* See what it says in the corner here? *Seal of Quality.* Seal of Quality, Tiger! Quality Seal Sausages! Real polar bear food! The supermarket, first thing tomorrow!'

Looks like the Hero's Funeral is off, and shopping is on.

'All right, Oscar. Whatever you want,' I sigh. 'Whatever you want.' What I do for that bear!

Chapter Twenty-three

Minus 20

'Oscar, I'm so sorry.' I can feel him shaking under my coat.

The meat counter man is laughing. 'You actually thought that a *Seal of Quality* meant that the sausages were made of …' and he laughs some more. '… *seal!* Don't you know that seals are a protected species? I'd go to prison if I sold you a seal sausage or a seal anything come to that. George, come over here and listen to this! There's a little girl wants seal sausages!'

I run off and crouch down behind a stash of trolleys.

'Oscar, I am so, so sorry.'

'I don't know which is worse,' groans Oscar, 'you not being **ghastly** anymore, or still not having seal to eat.'

'Oscar, I am so–'

'For goodness sake Tiger, can't you just be rude for a

minute. Listen, I want to go and join the others – now.'

'Well, the boys will still be messing around Fruit and Veg, and Mum will probably be over in Bakery – or Wine.'

'No, I don't mean – no listen, just take me to the lift.'

'The lift? The lift back up to the car park on the roof?'

'Yes, stupid. Now!'

At least Oscar is back to his normal rude self, which cheers me up, so I don't bother to ask him why.

We call the lift and get in. I am about to press the 1 button to go up, when Oscar growls:

'Wait!'

And he rips off the label that is taped over the bottom button, you know, the one that says

DO NOT PREZ THIS BURTON!

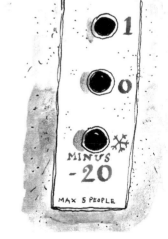

And then...   ...he presses it!

'Oscar, the button says *Minus 20*. Does that mean we are going 20 floors underground? Oscar, I'm frightened!'

Oscar puts his paw in my hand.

'Don't worry, Tiger, we're just going down one floor.'

'How do you know Oscar? Minus 20 floors must be halfway to Australia.'

'I know, because I wrote that sign!' says Oscar proudly. 'We're going into the huge storage freezer under the supermarket. It's kept at Minus 20 degrees, which is not as cold as the Frozen Arctic in winter, but it'll do.'

The lift stops with a clonk, but the doors don't open.

'Oscar, we're stuck!'

'Don't worry, Tiger. This entrance to the freezer isn't used any more, but one of the others will open it in a minute.'

And Oscar lets out a great big 'Gr r r r r r- or r r r' and starts knocking on the lift door.

'The others?' I say. 'Oscar, what's going on?' But Oscar ignores me and carries on thumping the door.

Suddenly the lift doors slide open. A thick cloud of icy fog pours out. And a strange smell. Like the one I got on my shoe near the iceberg.

'Oh hi, Wolf!' grunts Oscar. 'I'm back, and I've

brought a friend – Tiger - but she isn't one; but she's got big teeth and she's not for eating, OK?'

'Sure, Oscar,' barks Wolf – and it really is a wolf, the Arctic wolf. 'Welcome to *Minus 20!* Come on in and meet the others. Hey! You do have big teeth, Tiger! Classy! Almost as big as mine!' Wolf bears his teeth.

I grip Oscar's paw really tight and shiver as Wolf leads the way through swirling icy fog past rows of frosty boxes piled up to the ceiling.

'Mind your head on the icicles here,' he barks, but I know just what he is saying. Like with Oscar, it's easy to understand other creatures if you listen hard enough.

Out of the fog a reindeer appears. And then I make out an arctic fox sucking frozen chips, lying on top of an enormous hairy musk ox. A glaucous gull flies past with a battered cod in his mouth. 'Nice hair, kid!' it squawks, and drops the cod on my head.

And then something slithers out from behind a mountain of ripped apart boxes of fish fingers. It's a seal!

'What on earth are you all doing here?' I say, but my words come out all frozen and crash to the ground in

splinters. 'And why aren't you eating each other?'

They must be used to frozen words because they all seem to understand.

'Well it was all my idea,' grunts Oscar.

'No it wasn't, it was mine!' barks Wolf.

'It was OUR idea,' yelps Seal. 'All of us. We were trapped on an iceberg. We agreed to put all our individual Special Instincts together to survive. We wouldn't be alive now if we hadn't. Team Frozen we call ourselves. In fact…'

'Hey, Tiger is my friend,' growls Oscar. 'I'll tell her the story.'

Chapter Twenty-four

Trapped.

'So there we were,' says Oscar. 'Trapped on an iceberg. And all of us with one Special Instinct in common: all other creatures are either food or an enemy – or both. So I decided…'

'**We** decided,' chant all the other animals.

'All right then, we decided that each of us would be given the chance to say why we shouldn't be eaten.'

'I said that my Special Instinct was my eyesight,' says Glaucous Gull. 'Flying high in the sky I would be able to see where our iceberg was drifting.'

'And I said my Special Instinct was my sense of smell,' says Arctic Fox. 'And I would be able to smell the Frozen Arctic long before the Gull saw it.'

'And I said my Special Instinct was my howl,' says Wolf. 'And I could howl at night to warn ships not to crash into us.'

'And I said no-one could eat me,' snorts Reindeer. 'Because I work for Father Christmas, and it would be bad luck to chew me to bits.'

'And he kept us entertained,' says Arctic Fox. 'All through the long nights with tales of his adventures with Santa.'

'Very long tales,' bellows Muskox. 'Though why everyone stayed awake at night shivering and listening to Reindeer when I said they could all cuddle up under my long hair, what with my Special Instinct of being able to lie with my back to the wind even before the wind has made its mind which way to blow from.'

'My list of Special Instincts was very long, as you can imagine,' says Oscar.

'Which is why we told him to stop boasting and shut up or else, what with him being an exceptionally small and tasty-looking lump of flesh—' says Wolf.

Oscar looks at Wolf's big teeth but interrupts all the same: 'And I said if only they would let me eat Seal, I would become the biggest and strongest of all, and be able to dig comfortable snow-holes for us to hibernate in.'

'Then I said they couldn't feed me to Oscar,' says Seal. 'Because I was the best at catching fish, and without me they would all starve to death.'

'But we all knew that while Oscar is very small, very rude, very bad-mannered and very grumpy,' says Arctic Fox. 'He has a very big brain.'

'Which is why,' says Glaucous Gull, 'when our iceberg crashed into the harbour wall, Oscar was able to find Team Frozen a home here at *Minus 20.*'

'Until there's a gale blowing in the right direction to take us back to the Frozen Arctic,' says Oscar. 'And that's why I had to find somewhere to live where I could watch for the wind.'

'Meanwhile, we've been building *The Iceberg,*' barks Wolf, pointing at a raft made of wooden pallets and empty plastic bottles. 'Muskox and Reindeer are going to drag it down to the sea.'

'As soon as Oscar tells us that a gale-force southerly is on its way,' says Seal.

Oscar gives me a 'Don't Tell Them We've Missed It'

look.

'It's all my fault, I've let you all down…' I start to say, but I am shaking, and my tears are raining down like hailstones.

'For goodness sake, stop it!' growls Oscar. 'This is no place for a shivering, weepy Tiger. Thanks to you, I now know the best route to get the raft to the harbour without being seen. I always knew that a lump of melting ice wouldn't get us home. You've done your bit. You've not let us down. Now let's get you out of here.'

I nod, and, taking his paw, we set off through the freezing fog.

We stop in front of something solid. Oscar reaches up on tiptoes and rests my gloved hand on a big handle.

'I'd better get back to the team,' grunts Oscar. 'Just lift that handle and the door will open.'

I want to say all sorts of things to Oscar: a lot of *thank-yous* and *I'm sorrys*; and how much I want him to come home with me, and how much I'll miss him.

'I know what you're thinking, Tiger,' grunts Oscar. 'But you've done the right thing bringing me back.

Together, Team Frozen will survive. *The Iceberg* will get us home.'

'But us? What about us?' I say, reaching out to take his paw.

'I'll look out for a postman,' he grunts. 'And send you a postcard. You can come and visit.'

I want to hug him tight, but he's already strolling off, back to his Team. **Ghastly** Oscar in a Team!

He turns and waves a paw. 'So long! And thanks for all the fish fingers.'

Thanks? I can't believe it! Oscar said *Thanks!*

'I will,' I shout back at the disappearing bear. 'I will come!'

I push and push, but with only one good arm I can't shift the lift door handle. I collapse on the floor in a heap, too cold to cry, too cold to shout, too cold to think.

All I know is, I'm stuck. Stuck in *Minus 20*.

It's not Oscar and the Frozen Arctic animals who are trapped.

IT'S ME!

Chapter Twenty-five

Special instincts.

I am floating on an iceberg. The air is still and peaceful, and the sky full of stars.

Something shakes me by the collar and starts dragging me across the ice.

'Is that you Wolf?' I mumble.

'No it isn't, it's Patrick,' says Wolf. 'And I've come to rescue you.'

Then Seal slaps me on the face.

'Ouch! Your flipper is really hard, Seal.'

'I'm not a seal, I'm Henry. Wake up! We've got to get you into the lift.'

I look around. The stars have disappeared. The iceberg does look rather like a lift. And Wolf and Seal do look rather like Patrick and Henry.

'Where's Oscar then?' I ask.

'Oscar? Your fluffy toy's at home,' replies the Wolf who calls himself Patrick.

'We're having his Hero's Funeral this afternoon, remember?' says the Seal who calls himself Henry. 'We've done all the badges and medals.'

'The Hero's Funeral is off,' I say.

'Well, if we hadn't rescued you,' says Patrick. 'Tiger McDoo's Funeral would definitely have been on!'

'At least our badges and medals wouldn't have been wasted,' says Henry.

'So how did you find me down here?'

'We're triplets, Tiger. We're inseparable,' says Henry.

'We've got Triplets Special Instincts, haven't we?' says Patrick. 'We couldn't find you up in the supermarket. We **sensed danger**.'

'I **smelled** it,' says Henry.

'I **felt** it,' says Patrick. 'Then we both **heard** it.'

'We called the lift to go and look for you in the rooftop carpark,' says Henry. 'And we heard the lift coming **up** the lift shaft rather than coming **down**.'

'That's impossible, we thought,' says Patrick. 'There is

no more 'down' than the 0 button.'

'Then we saw the sign torn off, and a button that said *Minus 20*,' says Henry.

'We knew it had to be you, Tiger,' says Patrick. 'You're such an explorer.'

With a clunk, the lift starts up the shaft. The door opens and there is Mum.

'Tiger, what's happened to you?' cries Mum. 'Your lips are blue and you're shaking.'

Well, I could tell her the whole long story, but I settle for the short story.

'It's all right Mum, I've just been exploring the big freezer. I wanted to see what it's like in the Frozen Arctic 'cos I'm going to explore it for real one day.'

Mum carries me to the car and tells Henry and Patrick to snuggle up and warm me.

And I'm thinking: Team McDoo. We're triplets. We've got Special Instincts, too.

'We are inseparable, aren't we?' I say to my Hero Brothers. 'You know, I don't think I want a bedroom of my own. Not just yet, anyway.'

When we get home Mum pulls off my coat and scarf, and then hugs me.

'I love you Mum,' I say. 'And Dad.' And I mean it; but Mum isn't listening.

'Tiger! Your hair! What's this disgusting greasy stuff?'

'Oh that?' I say, casually. 'A glaucous gull flew past and dropped a battered cod on my head.'

'Tiger McDoo! If anyone else had said anything as ridiculous as that, I wouldn't for one moment have believed them. But with you Tiger, well the trouble with you is that … well, with you anything – absolutely anything – is possible.'

And I'm thinking, there are a lot of things worse than a battered cod that a glaucous gull could drop on your head.

It could have been worse than disgusting.

It could have been totally

and utterly…

ghastly!

Totally and utterly
the ghastly end.